# The Sugar Bear Story

Published in Cooperation with the Santa Barbara Museum of Natural History

SANTA BARBARA
MUSEUM OF NATURAL HISTORY

Inspiring a passion for the natural world.

The Sugar Bear Story

Story by Mary J. Yee **Illustrations by Ernestine Ygnacio-De Soto**

With contributions by Marianne Mithun, Ph.D. and John R. Johnson, Ph.D.

Sunbelt Publications

San Diego, California

Sunbelt Publications, Inc.
All rights reserved. First edition 2005
Edited by Jennifer Redmond
Book and cover design by Leah Cooper
Production Coordinator Jennifer Redmond
Printed in the United States of America

Sunbelt Publications, Inc.
P.O. Box 191126
San Diego, CA 92159-1126
(619) 258-4911, fax: (619) 258-4916
www.sunbeltbooks.com

08 07 06 05   5 4 3 2 1

Library of Congress Cataloging-in-Publication Data

  Yee, Mary J., b. 1897.
    The sugar bear story / story by Mary J. Yee; illustrations by Ernestine
Ygnacio de Soto ; with contributions by John R. Johnson and Marianne
Mithun.--1st ed.
        v. cm.
    Text in English and Chumash.
    Includes bibliographical references and index.
    Contents: Territory map -- Chumash history -- Chumash culture -- The
sugar bear story.
    ISBN-13: 978-0-932653-70-3
    ISBN-10: 0-932653-70-7
    1. Chumash Indians--Folklore. 2. Chumash language--Texts. [1. Chumash
Indians--Folklore. 2. Indians of North America--California--Folklore. 3.
Chumash language materials--Bilingual.] I. De Soto, Ernestine Ygnacio, ill.
II. Title.
    E99.C815Y44 2005
    398.2'089'9758--dc22
                        2005003047

Illustrations by Ernestine Ygnacio-De Soto

Table of Contents

Acknowledgements

This little book would not have been possible without the assistance of several individuals. Dr. Marianne Mithun, a specialist in American Indian languages at the University of California, Santa Barbara, checked over the linguistic accuracy of my interpretation of my mother's Barbareño Chumash text and contributed the vocabulary list and pronunciation guide. My friend Dr. John R. Johnson, Curator of Anthropology at the Santa Barbara Museum of Natural History, facilitated the process of bringing forth this book. Marie Murphy, Art Director at the Museum of Natural History, and Mike Carpenter assisted in putting my original drawings and design ideas onto the printed page. Jennifer Redmond of Sunbelt Publications ably guided us in making this book a reality, and Leah Cooper of Armadillo Creative added the finishing touches to our original design. Jennifer and Leah patiently worked with us to create an updated map and legend that accurately reflects our current understanding of the original linguistic relationships among the Chumash peoples and their neighbors. This publication was made possible in part through a grant received from the John and Beverly Stauffer Foundation. I would like to express my gratitude to all of the above for their contributions.

Ernestine Ygnacio-De Soto

Preface

When I was little, lying in the dark, I listened to the nightly bedtime stories told by my mother. Now that I am past my mother's age, I feel that the stories were for her as much as they were for me. They kept the memories of her Chumash childhood alive, as they filled mine.

The story of the **Sugar Bear** was not one that she told me, but I found it in her journals where she recorded her language and stories while she worked with the anthropologist and linguist John P. Harrington in the 1950s. This story has become near and dear to my heart because my mother loved bears and so do I.

Many Chumash stories carry the message of how you should behave in life. The moral of the **Sugar Bear Story** is how you should treat your guests.

Ernestine Ygnacio-De Soto
September 10, 2003

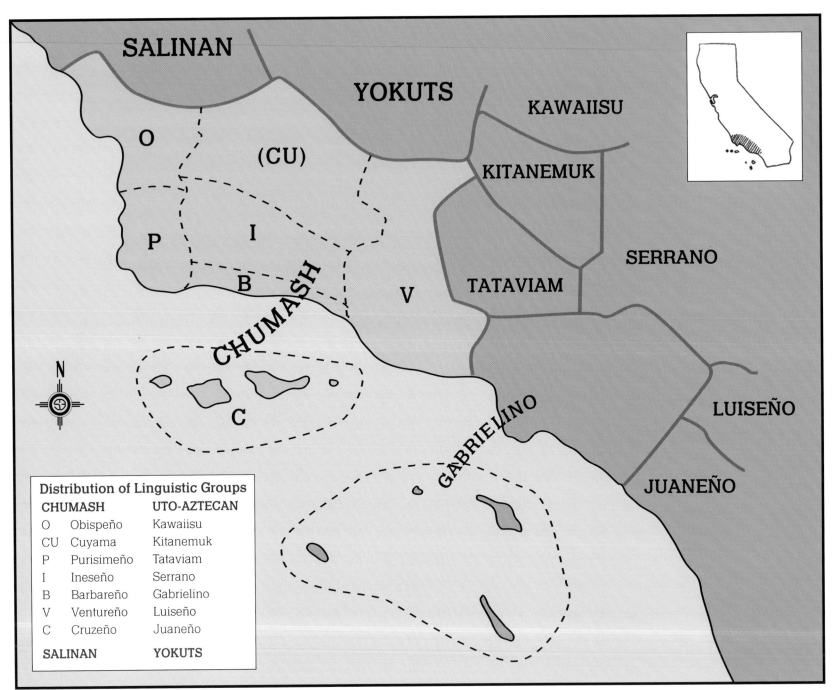

SALINAN

YOKUTS

KAWAIISU

O

(CU)

KITANEMUK

P

SERRANO

I

TATAVIAM

B

CHUMASH

V

C

GABRIELINO

LUISEÑO

JUANEÑO

N

Distribution of Linguistic Groups

CHUMASH		UTO-AZTECAN
O	Obispeño	Kawaiisu
CU	Cuyama	Kitanemuk
P	Purisimeño	Tataviam
I	Ineseño	Serrano
B	Barbareño	Gabrielino
V	Ventureño	Luiseño
C	Cruzeño	Juaneño
SALINAN		**YOKUTS**

Base map from *The Material Culture of the Chumash Interaction Sphere* (5 vols.), by Travis Hudson and Thomas Blackburn, Ballena Press, 1982-1987, Menlo Park, CA.

Chumash History

The homeland occupied by Chumash peoples was first settled some 13,000 years ago, according to archaeological evidence. Over time, the population increased and the people continued to adapt their way of life to the local environment. At the time of Juan Rodríguez Cabrillo's voyage in 1542, about 20,000 people lived throughout the territory where Chumash languages were spoken. Between 1772 and 1804, five missions were founded to convert the Chumash populations. The languages spoken in different parts of the Chumash region are now known by names taken from these missions: Obispeño, Purisimeño, Ineseño, Barbareño, and Ventureño.

By the end of the 62-year Mission Period, introduced European diseases had reduced the Chumash populations to a little more than 2,000. Despite these losses, Chumash communities persisted in the neighborhood of the former missions. Chumash Indians farmed their own lands or worked on ranches to support themselves. Some families, like the Ygnacio family into which Mary J. Yee was born, continued to speak their native language and preserve the stories handed down through the generations. Since the beginning of the twentieth century, the Chumash population has increased and more than 5,000 descendants live today in their former homeland.

Chumash Culture

"**C**humash" is the name of the American Indians who lived in about 150 towns and villages along the Central California coast and neighboring islands, mountains, and valleys. There were several different Chumash languages. The Barbareño language was once spoken along the Santa Barbara mainland coast between the present town of Carpinteria and Refugio State Beach. Chumash Indians lived off of the bounty of the sea and land, fishing, hunting, and gathering wild seeds and acorns. They are known for their skilled basket weaving, sea-going plank canoe or *tomol*, shell bead money, and their colorful rock paintings. Respect for nature and care of the land has always been part of Chumash life and religion. Storytelling is the way that Chumash Indians have passed on their culture and history to their children, as this little book demonstrates.

S-wil-waš hiʔ-l ayʔi

There was someone

1

hiʔ-l wil-waš hi s-qoʔ hiʔ-l xus

who had a bear as a pet.

S-qili-niwalˀik hi
s-wala-kumihas.

He used to
come running
all the time
in a bad mood

3

hi hoʔ s-ʔap
to his house

4

k'e s-qili-sili-ʔuw-š

and he used to want to bite people.

5

S-am-qili-api-yik-us
hi?-l mow

They used to
quickly give
him sugar

6

hi mal'i s-wala-kumi

as soon as he arrived

čo s-am-su-čʰo-l-us hi s-ʔantik.

to make him   happy.

Ču ka k-iy-qili-ʔip
And so we used to say

hi malʔi sʰ-aʔ-kumiˋ   hoʔ-l ʔap,

when someone is
coming to the house,

Grrr! ay'i hi'-l xu'wil, one who is angry,

"Su-ti-lekʔen-us hi hoʔ s-mow!"

"Quickly set his sugar down in front of him!"

Mary J. Yee

Born in 1897 at her grandmother's adobe home near Santa Barbara, Mary J. Yee was one of the few children of her generation to be brought up speaking a Chumash language. Being brought up in her grandmother's household until the age of twelve, she heard and committed to memory many old Chumash stories spoken in her native tongue. Many years later she was to write down these stories while working with the noted anthropologist John P. Harrington. This little book, illustrated by Mary Yee's daughter Ernestine, is one of those stories.

Mary J. Yee (1897-1965)

Ernestine Ygnacio-De Soto

A lifelong resident of Santa Barbara, Ernestine grew up listening to the Barbareño Chumash language being spoken by her mother and great-uncle. Throughout the day and as bedtime stories, she heard many Chumash tales recited in English by her mother. While making her living as a registered nurse, Ernestine finds the time to keep her culture and history alive through presenting Chumash public programs and collaborating with the Department of Anthropology at the Santa Barbara Museum of Natural History. Ernestine illustrated her mother's Sugar Bear story with its bilingual translation as an example of how life's lessons are transmitted to children in traditional Chumash society.

Photo courtesy of Kathleen Conti

Ernestine De Soto and Granddaughter

Vocabulary List

xus	. . . .	*bear*
qoʔ	. . . .	*pet*
s-qoʔ	. . . .	*his pet, her pet*
ʔap	. . . .	*house*
s-ʔap	. . . .	*his house, her house*
mow	. . . .	*sugar*
s-mow	. . . .	*his sugar, her sugar*
ʔantik	. . . .	*heart, spirit*
s-ʔantik	. . . .	*his heart or spirit, her heart or spirit*
s-ʔuw-š	. . . .	*he bites, she bites, it bites*
s-sili-ʔuw-š	. . . .	*he/she/it likes to bite*
s-qili-ʔuw-š	. . . .	*he/she/it used to bite*
s-qili-sili-ʔuw-š	. . . . . .	*he/she/it used to like to bite*

s-yik-us	. . . .	*he gives it to him*
s-api-yik-us	. . . .	*he quickly gives it to him*
s-qili-yik-us	. . . .	*he used to give it to him*
s-qili-api-yik-us	. . . . .	*he used to quickly give it to him*
k-yik-us	. . . .	*I give it to him*
k-api-yik-us	. . . .	*I quickly give it to him*
k-qili-yik-us	. . . .	*I used to give it to him*
k-qili-api-yik-us	. . . . .	*I used to quickly give it to him*
s-ʔip	. . . .	*he says, she says*
s-iy-ʔip	. . . .	*they say*
s-qili-ʔip	. . . .	*he used to say, she used to say*
s-iy-qili-ʔip	. . . .	*they used to say*

k-ʔip	. . . .	*I say*
k-qili-ʔip	. . . .	*I used to say*
k-iy-ʔip	. . . .	*we say*
k-iy-qili-ʔip	. . . .	*we used to say*
k-ʔip-us	. . . .	*I say to him or her, I tell him or her*
k-iy-ʔip-us	. . . .	*we tell him or her*
k-iy-qili-ʔip-us	. . . . . .	*we used to tell him or her*
k-iy-qili-sili-ʔip-us	. . .	*we used to want to tell him or her*
s-am-ʔip	. . . .	*someone says, people say*
s-am-qili-ʔip	. . . .	*someone used to say*
s-am-qili-ʔip-us	. . . . .	*someone used to tell him or her*
s-am-qili-sili-ʔip-us	. .	*somone used to want to tell him or her*

Pronunciation Guide

Vowels

The letters used to write Barbareño have about the same values as in Spanish.

a . . . . as in English f*a*ther
e . . . . as in English w*eigh*
i . . . . as in English p*i*zza
o . . . . as in English sm*o*ke
u . . . . . . as in English s*u*per

They can be heard in words in the *Sugar Bear Story*.

ˀ**ap** . . . . *house*
    sounds about like the beginning of
    English *operation*

kˀe . . . . *so*
    rhymes with English *okay*

hi . . . . . *the*
    sounds like English *he*

mow . . . *sugar*
    sounds like the English verb *mow*,
    as in *mow the lawn*.

xus . . . . *bear*
    rhymes with English *juice*

Consonants

Some of the consonants sound just like they do in English

h . . . . . . as in English *hat*
l . . . . as in English *let*
m . . . . . . as in English *met*
n . . . . . . as in English *net*
s . . . . . . as in English *set*
w . . . . . . as in English *wet*
y . . . . as in English *yet*

The sounds below are pronounced almost as in English, but without a puff of air.

p . . . . . . as in English *spin*
t . . . . as in English *stick*
k . . . . . . as in English *skip*

The sound spelled **c** is pronounced like **ts**, and that spelled **q** is pronounced almost like **k**, but further back in the mouth.

When these sounds are pronounced with an extra puff of air, as in English, the puff is shown with ʰ.

pʰ . . . . . . as in English *pin*
tʰ . . . . . . as in English *tick*
kʰ . . . . . . as in English *key*

The sound written **x** is something like **h** with more friction, or like the last sound in *Bach*.

There are also some special letters.

č . . . . like English *ch* in *chip*
š . . . . like English *sh* in *ship*

Finally, there are some sounds in Barbareño Chumash that are not exactly like any English sounds. These are the glottal stop ˀ and glottalized consonants like **pˀ, tˀ, cˀ, č, kˀ, qˀ**, and **lˀ, mˀ, nˀ, wˀ**, and **yˀ**. The glottal stop is like the sound in the exclamation *uh-oh*, meaning *woops*, or in some pronunciations of *bottle*. The other glottalized consonants are pronounced with a similar constriction in the throat. Something close to the sounds might be produced by pronouncing certain phrases very quickly, with special force on the second word: up **oút**, at **áll**, pa**ck** **úp**.

A Note About Languages

The language of this story, Barbareño Chumash, belongs to the Chumash language family. A language family is a group of languages that have all developed from the same parent language. The known languages of the Chumash family are Obispeño, Purisimeño, Ineseño, Barbareño, Ventureño, and Cruzeño (also called Island Chumash). Since these six languages all had their origins in the same parent language, they share certain similarities, much like English and German or Spanish and French. They are, however, separate languages, which means that they are mutually unintelligible. A Barbareño speaker, for example, could not understand a Ventureño speaker without learning Ventureño.

Most of the Chumash languages have several dialects. Speakers of different dialects of a language can understand each other, but their speech is not exactly the same. Different dialects of English are spoken in Santa Barbara and New Orleans, for example. Barbareño Chumash also had several dialects. Speakers from the Dos Pueblos area could easily converse with speakers from Syuxtun, near the present Santa Barbara wharf area, but each group would notice slight differences in the speech of the others, and perhaps be able to identify them right away just on that basis. The Ventureño language had a number of dialects as well: people from the communities around present Mugu, Malibu, Shisholop, Matilija, and the area around Ojai, Santa Paula, Sespe, and Castac, each had slightly different forms of speech. Cruzeño, the language spoken on the Channel Islands, also had several dialects. People from Santa Cruz Island could easily understand people from Santa Rosa Island, but they would know where they came from as soon as they heard them speak.

The Chumash languages show no demonstrable genetic relationship to the languages of their neighbors or any of those beyond. Their neighbors to the north spoke languages of the Salinan family and the Yokuts family.

Their neighbors to the east spoke languages of the Uto-Aztecan family: Gabrielino, Tataviam, Kitanemuk, and Kawaiisu. Because Chumash-speaking peoples did talk to their neighbors, they borrowed certain words, but the languages of the Chumash, Salinan, Yokuts, and Uto-Aztecan families all developed from different ancestral languages.

The common origin of the Chumash languages can be seen in many shared words and grammatical structures, features they all inherited from their common parent. Barbareño and Ineseño are so close that they are nearly dialects. Their closest neighbors, Purisimeño and Ventureño, are also quite similar. Obispeño, at the far north, and Cruzeño out on the islands, show the greatest differences. In this story, for example, we saw the Barbareño word **xus** *bear*. Words in the other Chumash languages are quite similar. We saw the word **kiyqili'ip** *we used to say*, composed of **kiy-** *we*, **-qili-** *used to*, and **'ip** *say*. The verb root *say* is nearly the same in the other languages. We also saw the word **s'ap** *his house*, composed of **s-** *his, her, or its* and **'ap** *house*. The noun root **'ap** *house* is the same in Ineseño, Barbareño, and Ventureño, but different in the others.

	bear	say	house
Obispeño	tuquski	'ipi	qhnipu
Purisimeño	axus	'ip	
Ineseño	xus	'ip	'ap
Barbareño	xus	'ip	'ap
Ventureño	xus	'ip	'ap
Cruzeño	xu'us	'i	'awa

— Dr. Marianne Mithun

Sunbelt Publications

Incorporated in 1988 with roots in publishing since 1973, Sunbelt produces and distributes publications about "Adventures in Natural History and Cultural Heritage of the Californias." These include natural science and outdoor guidebooks, regional histories and reference books, multi-language pictorials, and stories that celebrate the land and its people.

Sunbelt books help to discover and conserve the natural and historical heritage of unique regions on the frontiers of adventure and learning. Our books guide readers into distinctive communities and special places, both natural and man-made.

"In the end, we will conserve only what we love,
we will love only what we understand,
we will understand only what we are taught."

— Bouba Dioum, Senegalese conservationist

Suggested Reading List

www.sunbeltbooks.com